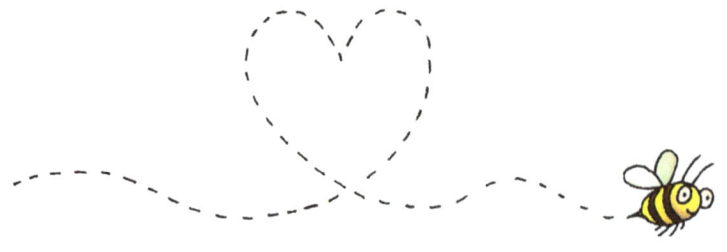

**Dedicated to my son Sam
and my dog Chloe.
With love, appreciation and gratitude,
Mom**

All of the information contained in this book is presented for informational and artistic purposes only. Any person should use caution and appropriate supervision and training doing all poses in this book. The publisher is not responsible for any accidents, injuries or damages suffered by any reader of this book.

Text copyright (c) 2018 by Stacey Alysson
Illustrations copyright (c) 2018 by Patrick Girouard

Published in 2018 by Stacey Alysson Yoga. All rights reserved. No portion of this book may be reproduced, stored in a retrieval system, or transmitted in any form or by any means, mechanical, electronic, photocopying, recording, or otherwise, without written permission from the publisher.

Stacey Alysson Yoga | 9663 Santa Monica Boulevard #1136 | Beverly Hills, CA 90210

ISBN 9780692112137
ISBN 978-0-692-11213-7

www.ParkerPigGoestoYoga.com

Every morning, Parker Pig laid in the sun, but today was going to be different. Today was going to be yoga class with all of Parker's new friends.

In the distance, Parker saw Ginny Giraffe walking towards her and she excitedly jumped up, grabbed her yoga mat and raced over to greet Ginny!

"Good morning, Parker! It's a beautiful day to go to the beach."

Parker confusedly responded, "Ginny, we can't do yoga on the beach." "Of course we can, Parker! We can do yoga anywhere." "What a great idea, Ginny! Ok, let's go" Parker exclaimed.

Parker and Ginny arrived at the beach where the sun shined brightly and gentle waves crashed along the ocean shore.

Walking along the beach and snapping her giant red claw was Charli Crab. Ginny started class by saying, "Let's sit down in the sand and pose like a reverse table top for CRAB POSE."

SNAP SNAP

In the distance, jumping out of the glistening ocean, was Darren the Dolphin. "Put your forearms in the sand and lift your hips up to the sky for DOLPHIN POSE."

WHOSH WHOSH

Swimming around Darren Dolphin in a circle was Sam the Shark. "Lay down on your belly and press your palms together behind your back like a shark fin for SHARK POSE!" SWISH SWISH

Riding the rolling waves above Sam the Shark was Stan the Surfer. "Stand up and jump your legs apart. Reach your arms out, put a bend in your knee, and balance your body on your mat for SURFER POSE."

I AM STRONG

Resting quietly along on the rocks was Sloane the rainbow-colored Starfish enjoying the serene sounds of the ocean around her. "Lay down on your back and spread your arms and legs out for STARFISH POSE."

AHHH AHHH

Laying calmly and still next to Sloane the Starfish, was Cade the Clam.

"Lay on your side as you calmly and slowly open and close your leg for CLAMSHELL POSE."

HI, CLAMS

In the soft warm sand, Marijke the Mermaid was swishing her brightly colored shiny tail to the right and to the left, extending her arm up and over with each deep breath in and out. "Grow tall and shine as you twist your tail to the right and to the left for MERMAID POSE."

SPLASH SPLASH

Behind them in the distance was Mia the Mountain stretching out her beautiful arms made of trees.

"Lift your arms up to the sky and grow your body tall, pressing your palms together for MOUNTAIN POSE."

MOUNTAIN POSE

As Ginny and Parker practiced yoga, they noticed the sun was going down. They looked up in the sky, and could see a tiny slice of Benny the banana-shaped moon happily smiling down upon them.

"Breathe in and breathe out as you exhale to the right and to the left for BANANA MOON."

BANANA MOON

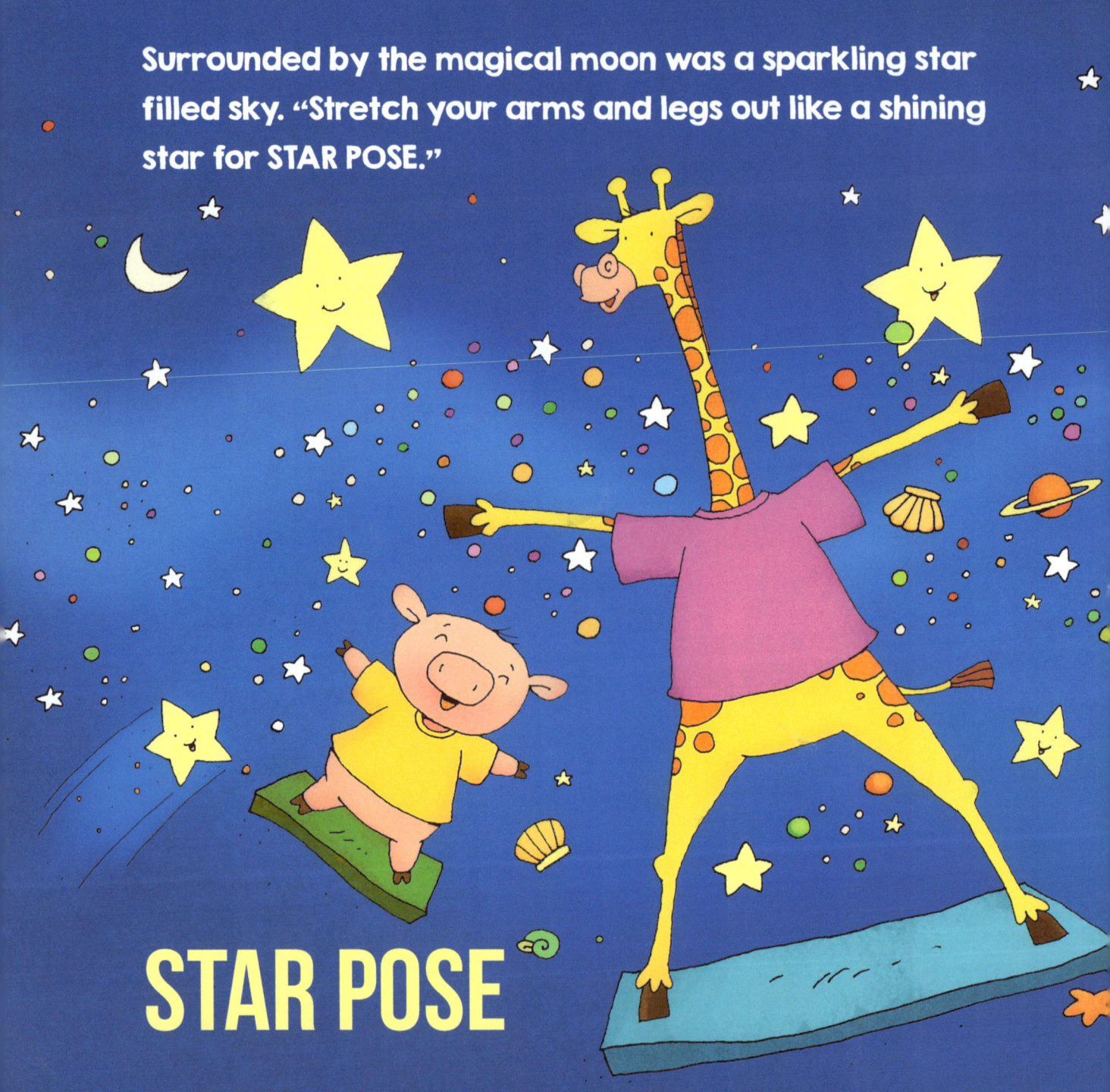

As they listened to the sounds in nature around them, they heard Henry the Horse galloping along the beach. "Squat down and press your palms together gracefully for HORSE POSE."

NAHH NAHH

Then, they looked up and saw Ben the Bee peacefully buzzing along the beach.

"Sit on your heels and take a deep breath in and out as you round your spine for BEE POSE." **BUZZZ BUZZZ**

Parker and Ginny laid down on their backs at the end of their yoga class for their final resting pose. "Lay down on your back with your arms and legs by your side. Keep your body completely still and relax for SAVASANA."

RELAX.

Ginny and Parker started to wiggle their fingers and toes as they reached their arms overhead. They slowly rolled onto their sides and sat all the way up for EASY POSE.

BREATHE IN AND BREATHE OUT

They pressed their hands together at their hearts and said, "The light in me honors and sees the light in you, and together we say, **NAMASTE!**"

Parker Pig was grateful for all her new beach yoga friends. After yoga, she felt happier, more relaxed and calm. Suddenly, she realized she could practice yoga anywhere, anytime and with anyone... including the beach!

She couldn't wait to see where she and Ginny would practice yoga next!

THE END.

Author

Stacey Alysson, the author of "Parker Pig Goes to Yoga," has returned with another interactive children's yoga book, "Parker Pig Goes to Beach Yoga." Stacey Alysson is a certified yoga instructor and Mom. She is passionate about teaching children and sharing the gift of yoga through storytelling, specializing with children 2 to 8 years of age.

Illustrator

When Patrick Girouard was growing up his teachers constantly scolded him for drawing monsters and aliens during class. Then, he finished growing up and illustrated his first book. It was about monsters!

Now his work can be found in children's books, museum exhibits, magazines, greeting cards, t-shirts, games, toys, puzzles, odd scraps of paper, the margins of newspapers, and his Mom's refrigerator door.

CPSIA information can be obtained
at www.ICGtesting.com
Printed in the USA
LVHW02n0025080618
579199LV00004BD/7/P